THE HOUND OF ULSTER

White Wolves Series Consultant: Sue Ellis,
Centre for Literacy in Primary Education

This book can be used in the White Wolves Guided Reading
programme with more experienced readers at Year 4 level

First published 2007 by
A & C Black Publishers Ltd
38 Soho Square, London, W1D 3HB

www.acblack.com
www.malachydoyle.co.uk

Text copyright © 2007 Malachy Doyle
Illustrations copyright © Mike Phillips

ISBN 978-0-7136-8194-9

A CIP catalogue for this book is available from the British Library.

This book is produced using paper that is made from wood grown
in managed, sustainable forests. It is natural, renewable and
recyclable. The logging and manufacturing processes conform
to the environmental regulations of the country of origin.

Printed and bound in Great Britain by MPG Books Limited.

THE HOUND OF ULSTER

Malachy Doyle
Illustrated by Mike Phillips

A & C Black • London

To Louis Isaac Cuchulainn,
he of the bark most tuneful

CONTENTS

CHAPTER ONE
SETANTA'S DREAM

Setanta always knew that he was different.

"I'm going to be famous," he boasted to his mother, when he was only six years old. "I'm going to be a Red Branch Knight!"

"Don't be silly, child," said his mother, laughing. "For one thing you're too young, for a second you're too skinny and for a third you're too poor."

Setanta was sad, then, but his mother put her arm around him. "Only the sons of noblemen become warriors, love," she told him. "The great king of Ulster, Conor Mac Nessa, would never have one such as you! You'll grow up to be a shepherd, like your father. Now fetch me some wood for the fire and put such thoughts from your mind."

But Setanta wouldn't give up on his dream. His father often spoke of the band of boys that the king had brought together at Emain Macha, the Red Branch headquarters, to train up as his champions. The young warriors were great hurlers, and specially chosen for their skill at games and sports.

So Setanta made himself a hurley stick from the branch of an ash tree, and found a round stone to use as a ball. As well as the hurley, he made himself a javelin and a spear, a shield and a sword, and he spent every free moment practising, until he was sure that he was just as good as the famous band of boys.

Then, one night, when his father was preparing to take their sheep down to the market in Emain Macha, Setanta crept up behind him.

"Could I go with you tomorrow, Father?" he asked.

"It's too far, boy," said the man. "You'll get tired, and I'll have to carry you."

"I won't," said Setanta. "I can run for miles."

"It's too busy," said his father. "I'll lose you in the crowd."

"You won't," said Setanta. "I'll stay close by."

"I've too much to do," said his father. "It's hard enough work keeping the sheep together, without having to watch out for a rascal like you."

But Setanta's mother took pity on him. "Oh, let him go with you, husband! He'll have to learn how to drive the sheep one day, so now's as good a time as any."

Setanta ran over and hugged her, for this was the moment he'd been dreaming of.

He hardly got a wink of sleep all night he was so excited and, by the first light of dawn, when his father came to wake him, he was already up and dressed.

They had a quick bite to eat, gathered the sheep, and set off on their way. It was a long journey,

sure enough, but Setanta ran on
ahead of the flock, playing at
games to shorten the way.

He whacked a stone into the
air with his hurley, as high and
hard as he could,
tossing the stick
after it. Running
forward, he caught
the hurley, held it
out and trapped
the stone on it.
The whole way to
Emain Macha, Setanta did this.
He never tired and he never
dropped the stone, not once.

When they arrived in the town, Setanta saw the king's boys, every one of them, practising their skills on the green. So, with a whoop and a holler, he ran to join them.

For now was the time to prove that the son of a poor shepherd was good enough to become a warrior of the mighty king.

CHAPTER TWO
THE YOUNG WARRIORS

Now Conor Mac Nessa, the king of Ulster, was greatly loved by all. He would often go to visit his chiefs and spend time in their houses feasting, which was how he got to know his people, and how they came to love him so well.

There was one man, named Culann, who the king had not got around to visiting yet, but who wished, more than anything,

for his lord and master to eat
and sleep in his house. He had
no great wealth, for he was a
blacksmith by trade, but he had
gone to the palace only the day
before and begged the king to
come and visit.

"I would be pleased to do so," replied the king, much to the blacksmith's delight. "I shall come tomorrow."

On the way to Culann's house the following morning, King Conor stopped by the green to watch his young warriors at play. He was surprised, though, as the

ball rose high into the air, to see a
strange boy, much smaller than
the rest, rushing on to the field.

With incredible skill for one so
young, Setanta caught the ball on
the edge of his stick, dodged round
the others, slipped it past them
and scored a wonderful goal.

The king was impressed, and wondered who the child was, for he was sure that he had never set eyes on him before.

But his young warriors were angry with the stranger for joining in their game uninvited, and even more so for showing them up in front of their lord and master.

They were determined to make it hard on the intruder from then on, and used every trick they knew to take the ball away from him.

Setanta, though, was faster than any one of them. He used his size to his advantage, dashing in and out between their legs, collecting the ball and racing with it down the field. Once he'd got the ball, there was no chance of taking it off him, for he'd dart and weave around like he'd been playing all his life. When it came to scoring, Setanta never missed once and, when the young warriors put him

in goal to keep him quiet, he
stopped every shot.

"Who do you think you are,
shepherd's boy?"
cried the tallest
of the king's
warriors,
furious with
the stranger
for making
him look slow-
footed and stupid.
"You can't just parade
on to the field and join in our
game without even asking. It is
an insult to us and to the king!"

He raised his stick and was about to knock Setanta to the ground, but the smaller boy was too quick for him. He sliced his own hurley low to the grass, chopping the proud fellow's legs out from under him, and it was the leader of the young warriors who ended up on his back.

There were one or two giggles, which made the boy on the ground even angrier.

"Attack him!" he yelled, and the others began flinging their hurleys at the intruder.

Setanta managed to duck out of the way so that not one of them struck him. They threw their balls at him instead, but Setanta used his arms and his feet to block them and to kick them out of sight.

"I'll sort that farmer's boy out once and for all!" cried the tallest of the young warriors, running to the side of the field to pick up his spear.

And he might have killed Setanta there and then, but for a great cry splitting the air.

CHAPTER THREE
BIG TALK

"HALT!" roared the king. And everyone stopped.

"Come here, child," he ordered, calling the unknown boy to his side. "What is your name and how old are you?"

"My name is Setanta, my lord," answered the boy. "I'm nearly seven, and I want to be one of your warriors."

"Where are you from, child?" asked the king. "For I've never seen you round here."

Setanta told him that he lived over the hills, and that he had come with his father to sell sheep in the market.

"You're a bit young to leave home and train to be one of my warriors, Setanta," laughed the king, finding his good humour again. "But you are brave for nearly seven, and if you prove to be as impressive a man as you are a boy, you may well have it in you to become a great warrior. If you will agree to let the others in my school look after you, I will consider allowing you to join."

"I don't need anyone to look after me!" cried Setanta. "I'm stronger and braver than any one of them!"

"Maybe you are," said the king, smiling. "But you are young, and I need to know you will be safe. It is one of my rules that any newcomer must ask the older boys to look out for him in times of trouble."

"Well, I'll change the rules!" insisted Setanta, scowling at the others. "I'll throw every one of them to the ground until they beg *me* to look after *them*!"

"It wouldn't surprise me if you did," replied the king, delighted at the boy's fierceness, "but I'm afraid I won't be able to watch, for I am on my way to a feast. Why not leave your fighting until another day and come along with me, for I am most impressed by your strength and courage."

"I'd be honoured, my lord," Setanta answered, "but I can't go until I've fought these boys and proved that I'm worthy to serve you."

"Fair enough," said the king, chuckling at the boy's pride. "It is a valiant task for a lad of your size, and I wish you luck. I will see you later, Setanta, if you are fit enough to follow after all your fighting. I am going with my men to the house of Culann the blacksmith. Do you know where he lives?"

"I don't, my lord," Setanta said. "But I'll have no trouble finding you, for as soon as I'm done here, I'll follow the marks of your horses' hooves."

King Conor sent word to
Setanta's father, so he would know
where his son was, and then he
and his men rode on to Culann's
house. There, they were made
welcome and a wonderful
banquet was laid out
before them.

As they sat down to eat, Culann the blacksmith came up to the king. "Is all your party present, my lord?" he asked. "Or are more coming later?"

"They are all here," said Conor, for his mind was on the food and drink before him and he'd already forgotten about the brave boy he'd told to follow on behind. "Why do you ask?"

"I have a fierce watchdog
to guard my land," Culann
explained. "It is a savage beast
that was brought from Spain and
it would take three chains, each
held by three men, to hold it down.
When I let it loose, no one dares
come near, and it will answer to
no man but me."

"It is safe to
let it off," said
the king, with
a mug of beer
in one hand
and a chicken
leg in the other.
"We are all inside."

So Culann went out, released the hound from its chains, and went back in to the feast. The beast, more like a wolf than a dog, bounded round the walls, barking ferociously to warn off any strangers.

The musicians inside played a little louder so the king was not disturbed by the howling. And, in time, when the creature was convinced there was no one about, it lay down on a grassy mound, where it could keep an eye out for anything that might threaten the safety of its master.

It remained there, with its head on its paws, alert to every movement, every smell and every sound.

Chapter Four
Setanta And The Beast

Setanta set out alone for Culann's house, following the horses' tracks along the road.

The fighting was over and, despite the fact that he was a whole heap smaller than they were, every one of the young warriors had ended up begging him for mercy.

To make the journey go
more quickly, Setanta
played with his stone,
whacking it up with
the hurley, flinging
the stick after it and
catching them both
as they fell.

When he drew near to Culann's house, he saw the candlelight shining from the windows of the hall and the shadowy outline of the king and his men as they feasted.

"Soon I'll be joining them," he said, and his stomach rumbled, for it had been a long, hard day, with little to eat.

But the ferocious guard dog, whose ears were trained to pick up the slightest sound, heard him muttering away to himself, and let out the sort of howl that would freeze your blood just to hear it.

Setanta, though, was far too excited to be put off his stride by the yowl of a dog. He was looking forward to feasting with the king, and telling him how he'd thrown every last one of his young warriors to the ground.

"He'll let me join his merry band of boys, and I'll be a Red Branch Knight in no time at all!" he muttered happily.

Finding the gate locked, he began climbing over the wall of the enclosure, but the fearsome hound had already spotted him. It licked its lips, gave a low growl, and prepared to pounce.

The moment Setanta hit the ground, he spotted the beast out of the corner of his eye, and couldn't help but gasp at the sight. Stopping dead in his tracks, he fingered his hurley and his stone,

for they were the only weapons
he carried, and turned to face the
ferocious creature. The hound
bared its teeth and sprang
at him, its jaws
gaping wide.

But with a roar that matched that of the beast, Setanta aimed his stone and flung it deep into the animal's throat. Then, as the creature lay gasping for breath, the boy caught hold of its head and beat it against a rock.

The musicians stopped playing just as the creature howled its final savage roar. Hearing the sound, a chill ran through the king's heart.

"Alas!" he cried to his men. "We should never have come here!"

"Why do you say such a thing, my lord?" asked Culann, shocked and offended.

"That bloodcurdling sound we have just heard," said the king, "has reminded me that I asked a brave young lad to follow me to your homestead. All I have done is lead him into the jaws of a wolf!

Run outside, men," he cried, "and see if you can do anything to save the life of that poor innocent child!"

CHAPTER FIVE
CUCHULAINN

The Ulstermen pulled out their weapons and dashed for the door, but when they got outside, all was silent. Nothing moved in the darkness and they crept around the enclosure, fearful that the hound might come upon them instead.

Then a small voice broke the stillness. "It's all right. I've killed it!"

A guard ran towards the voice
and found the dog lying dead on
the ground, and the boy standing
over its body.

"Thank the stars!" cried the guard, lifting Setanta up onto his shoulders and carrying him back into the hall, where the king sat with his head in his hands, expecting to hear the worst.

The guard put the boy at
the feet of the king and Conor
looked down in astonishment.
Then Setanta told him what
had happened. The assembled
company cheered the boy for his
courage, and the king hugged
and praised him.

But Culann the blacksmith was not so pleased. While everyone else was drinking a toast to the brave Setanta, the owner of the house went out into the yard and wept over the broken body of his dog.

"It's a bad day for my family," he lamented, when he got back inside. "We needed that hound to guard our land and keep us safe, and I will never be able to afford another like it.

You were right, Conor Mac Nessa," he continued, "I should never have invited you here, for look at the sadness and danger it has brought to me and my family."

The blacksmith turned to Setanta. "Young boy," he said, grimly. "You are welcome here for the king's sake, but not your own, for you have taken a good friend from me this day – one who served me well. Without that faithful hound, my wife and children will be unable to sleep soundly in their beds."

"I am most sorry, sir, that
I had to kill your dog," said
Setanta, "but it would have torn
me to pieces if I had not! What
can I do to help you?"

"How can a child such as you
help me?" cried the blacksmith.

"I could guard your house and lands, until you can find another hound to take its place," suggested Setanta.

"I have never heard of a young boy act as a guard dog!" cried the king, roaring with laughter. "But if such a thing is possible then I suppose you are the one to do it, for you are the fiercest, bravest boy I have ever met. You shall serve our host until I can replace his dog for him."

"There is no beast like it," said the blacksmith, sadly. "It can never be replaced."

"It is through my greed and my forgetfulness that you have lost your protector," said the king. "I shall scour the land, therefore, until I find one of the same breed. I shall have it reared and trained until it is at least as good as the one that died here tonight."

"That is a fair price, indeed," said Culann, nodding.

The king turned to Setanta. "To mark your courage and strength, child, from this day forward you shall be called Cuchulainn, the Hound of Culann. You will grow to be a great warrior and, in time, the men of Ireland and Scotland shall hear tell of your deeds and fear shall run through their bones."

Cuchulainn took great pride in the name he had been given, and for many years he watched over the blacksmith's house and lands, until the dog that the king found and trained was ready to replace the one he had killed.

No raider or wild animal dared go near while Cuchulainn was on guard, for he was as ferocious in his defence of the man's property as any beast could ever be, and the blacksmith and his family felt safe.

Then Conor Mac Nessa invited Cuchulainn to come and live in his palace. The boy joined the king's young warriors and, in the fullness of time, became leader of the Red Branch Knights.

He became a great champion of the king, famous through the whole of Ireland for his skill and his fighting. And he was known for the rest of his long and celebrated life as Cuchulainn, the Hound of Ulster.

Early Irish literature is divided into four main cycles: the Mythological, the Ulster, the Fenian and the Historical. The story of Cuchulainn belongs to the Ulster Cycle, which tells of the heroic exploits of Conor Mac Nessa and the Red Branch Knights, who are supposed to have lived around the time of the birth of Christ. Cuchulainn is the most famous character in this cycle, and most of the action takes place in the hill fort of Emain Macha and along the borders of the province of Ulster.

About The Author

Malachy Doyle grew up in a little town near Belfast. After spells as a Polo Mint packer, an advertisting executive and a Special Needs teacher, he now writes full-time.

Malachy has written more than 60 books, from pop-ups to teenage novels. He has a great fondness for folk tales, and the story of Cuchulainn has always been one of his favourites.

You can find out more about Malachy and his books on www.malachydoyle.co.uk.

Other White Wolves from
different cultures...

The Little
Puppet Boy

James Riordan

Petrushka the clown is the crowd's
favourite. But the little puppet boy
is unhappy. He's fed up with just
making people laugh. He longs to
be big and brave, like Strongman,
so he can save Pretty Ballerina
and take her away with him. All
he needs is courage. Will he find it?

The Little Puppet Boy is a well
known tale from Russian folklore.

ISBN: 9 780 7136 8213 7 £4.99

Other White Wolves from
different cultures...

The Story Thief

Andrew Fusek Peters

Nyame the sky god has a special
treasure – in a big, brass chest are
all the stories ever told. Anansi, the
cleverest of spiders, sees the people on
Earth are bored. She can't spin a tale,
but she can spin a web. So she makes a
ladder up to the sky, determined to get
back the stories, whatever it takes...

The Story Thief is a well known tale
from African folklore.

ISBN: 9 780 7136 8421 6 £4.99